P9-DCC-040

for Jonathan

I'll Teach My Dog 100 Words

I'll Teach My Dog 100 Words

by Michael Frith

Illustrated by

P. D. Eastman

A Bright & Early Book

From BEGINNER BOOKS
A Division of Random House, Inc., New York

Printed in Versailles, Kentucky U.S.A.   SP20000435NOV2012

Library of Congress Cataloging in Publication Data: Frith, Michael K. I'll teach my dog 100 words. (A Bright & early book)
SUMMARY: A youngster plans all the things he will teach his puppy.   [1. Stories in rhyme]   I. Eastman, Philip D.,
illus.   II. Title. PZ8.3.F918I1   [E]   73-2296 ISBN 0-394-82692-2 ISBN 0-394-92692-7 (lib. bdg.)

I'll teach my dog 100 words.

The first six words
I'll teach my pup
are . . .

dig a hole!

And
fill it up!

I'll teach him . . .

walk

and run,

and then . . .

catch a ball!

Now that makes ten.

And Mr. Smith,
who lives next door,
will say, "That's great!
Can you
teach him more?"

And then I'll teach him . . .

bark

and
beg

and
wag your tail

and
shake a leg. . . .

and
wash your ears

and
wash your toes

and
scratch your head
and
blow your nose!

Then Mr. Smith
will tell
Miss Brown,
"This is
the smartest
dog in town!"

I won't stop there.
No, not at all . . .

I'll teach him big,

I'll teach him small . . .

and fat and thin

and short and tall . ...

and dark . . .

and light . . .

and day . . .

and night.

And then
Miss Brown
will call
Miss May.
"Come over
right away,"
she'll say.

"This dog
is learning
chase the cat
and
climb the tree
and
things like that!"

Then we will give them more
to see . . .

eat your food

and follow me

Wow!
We're up to
forty-three.

I'll teach him

RED and BLUE and GREEN

"The smartest dog we've ever seen!"

I'll teach him

ORANGE
PURPLE
PINK

That makes forty-nine, I think.

And then Miss May
will call Mayor Meer.
She'll call,
"Please
hurry
over here!"

And then for Mr. Meer,
the Mayor,
I'll teach my dog . . .
now paint the chair!

Paint the road from here
to there

Then Mr. Meer, the Mayor, will say,
"I'll make today a holiday!"

And everyone will come to see
my amazing dog and me.

We'll show
them skate   and
                    kick the stone!

Jump the fishbowl!

Bring
the bone!

Chew the boot,
and hold the phone!

Cut the grass!

Shine my shoe!

Comb your hair!

And clean the zoo!

Now
brush the bear!

That's
eighty-two.

But that's not all my dog will do.

He'll tickle the pig,

and kiss the goose!

He'll feed the mouse,

and mop the moose!

He'll
toot a bugle . . .

beat a drum

He'll stand on
Uncle Abner's thumb

And then
I'll teach him
sing with
the birds

Now, THERE!
That makes
100 words.

My dog will learn
those hundred words—
and how my friends will cheer!

I'll teach my dog
those hundred words. . .

. . . I think I'll start next year.